THE DUCHESS AND THE GARDENER

A 19TH CENTURY ERA EROTIC SHORT STORY

ELIZA FINCH

1

_____

The grandiose bedroom of the Hawthorne estate lay shrouded in darkness, save for the flickering glow of a single candle that cast shadows upon the walls. Victoria, the Duchess of Hawthorne, sat on the edge of the massive bed, her delicate hands clasped together in her lap. The room was quiet, since her husband, the Duke of Hawthorne, died, the quiet was almost daunting. Despite the warmth from the fireplace, she felt an icy chill run down her spine, realizing the reality of her life – one filled with misery and unfulfilled desires.

"Is there anything else you need, madame? the maid asked.

"No, thank you," Victoria replied, her voice barely a whisper. She had only been married to the Duke for a few years. He was a man more than twice her age. Their marriage had been arranged by her family, a union of convenience rather than love. The Duke's wealth and status had been the driving force behind the arrangement, but deep down, she knew that there would be a price to pay for such security.

And now he was gone. His age and poor health had rendered

him unable to fulfill her desires, leaving Victoria with a growing sense of resentment and longing.

Determined to find solace and pleasure elsewhere, Victoria made up her mind. With her husband now gone, then perhaps it was time to seek out other dalliances. After all, a woman like her, blessed with youth and beauty, deserved more than a life of silent desperation.

"Goodnight, madame," the maid said before leaving the room.

"Goodnight," Victoria murmured, her mind racing with thoughts of passion and pleasure. As she lay alone in her bed, she vowed to herself that she would pursue her desires, even if it meant risking everything in the process. After all, what good was a life without passion?

Lost in her thoughts, Victoria hardly noticed the weight of the blankets that covered her body or the delicate lace that adorned her nightgown. Instead, she focused on the soft beating of her own heart, as she began to dream of the adventures that awaited her beyond the walls of the Hawthorne estate.

A SOFT BREEZE rustled the leaves of the ancient oak trees as Victoria strolled through the vast gardens of the Hawthorne estate. The warm sun caressed her porcelain skin, and she reveled in the sensation. She needed this time alone to clear her mind and escape the stifling confines of her life as a young widow.

As she rounded a corner, her gaze fell upon an unfamiliar figure. A young man, perhaps no older than twenty-five, stood among the rose bushes, his muscular arms glistening with sweat as he toiled under the sun. His name was Thomas, the newest addition to the estate's staff. Though he was a mere gardener, there was an unmistakable air of nobility about him.

"Good day," Victoria called out, her voice sweet and sultry.

Thomas looked up, momentarily startled by her presence. His dark eyes met hers, and for a moment, time seemed to stand still.

"Good day, miss," he replied, wiping the sweat from his brow with the back of his hand. He didn't recognize her as the Duchess, and Victoria found that fact both thrilling and liberating.

"Have you been working here long?" she asked coyly, taking a few steps closer to him. "I don't believe I've had the pleasure of meeting you before."

"Only a few days, miss," Thomas answered, his eyes lingering on the curve of her ample bosom, barely concealed beneath the delicate fabric of her gown.

"Ah, well then, welcome to Hawthorne estate," she purred, her heart pounding with anticipation. Her cheeks flushed with desire as she boldly locked her gaze with his. "I must say, it's always lovely to see such... strong, capable hands tending to the garden."

"Thank you, miss," Thomas murmured, his voice laced with seduction. He took a step towards her, closing the distance between them. He could feel the heat radiating off her body, and it stirred something primitive within him.

"Tell me," Victoria continued, her voice barely a whisper as she reached out to graze her fingers along his forearm. "Do your hands possess the same skill in other... pursuits?"

Thomas grinned wickedly, allowing himself to be drawn into her web of temptation. "Perhaps, miss," he replied, capturing her hand and drawing it to his lips. "Would you care for a demonstration?"

With a wicked gleam in his eye, Thomas pulled Victoria closer to him, their bodies barely touching as he whispered, "Very well, miss. Allow me the honor of demonstrating my talents."

Victoria's heart raced, and she could feel her body trembling with anticipation at this brazen display of passion. She had never imagined herself so bold, yet the thrill of the unknown stirred within her a wild desire that could not be tamed.

"Please," she breathed, her eyes locked on his as she offered herself up to him.

As if possessed by some primal force, their lips met in a searing kiss that sent shockwaves coursing through their entwined bodies. Victoria moaned into Thomas' mouth, her hands reaching up to explore the strong, muscular planes of his chest. She felt his breath catch as her fingers grazed the hard contours of his body, a testament to the countless hours he had spent laboring in the gardens.

"God, you're beautiful," Thomas growled, his voice thick with lust as he traced the outline of her full breasts with his rough, calloused hands. He deftly undid the buttons of her bodice, freeing her delicate flesh from its confines and allowing his greedy fingertips to roam uninhibited across her sensitive skin.

"Touch me, Thomas," Victoria gasped, her legs quivering with need as she urged him onward. She guided his hand lower, the expert touch of his fingers eliciting an electrifying pleasure that left her desperate for more.

"Such a sweet, eager little minx you are," he murmured, the crude words only serving to heighten her arousal. As his hand continued its tantalizing journey, she clung to him, her nails digging into the sinewy muscles of his back.

"Thomas, I need..." she panted, unable to form a coherent thought as her body writhed with ecstasy.

"Shh, I know, my sweet," he replied, his voice husky with desire. "You needn't say a word."

Just as their passion reached a fever pitch, the sound of approaching footsteps echoed through the garden, jolting them back to reality. They tore themselves apart, their eyes wide with panic as they scrambled to restore some semblance of decency before they were discovered.

Victoria quickly jumped behind a hedge to conceal herself. The head gardener George appeared.

"Thomas, what are you doing? Have you finished trimming the roses yet?"

"Almost sir," Thomas replied.

"Well hurry it along, I have more work for you to do on the other side of the gardens."

"Yes sir."

And with that, George left.

Victoria emerged from the hedges slowly and quietly.

"I'll look for you tonight," she whispered to Thomas. And then she quickly ran off so as not to be seen.

2
_____

Victoria's heart raced as she stealthily made her way back to the manor, unseen by any prying eyes. The thrill of stealing a passionate kiss from Thomas, the new gardener, left her feeling alive and excited in a way she hadn't experienced in years. Her cheeks flushed with a mix of arousal and embarrassment, as she knew that such an act was scandalous for a woman of her status.

"Damn propriety," she muttered under her breath, her pulse quickening at the memory of Thomas's strong, calloused hands gripping her waist during their illicit embrace.

Upon reaching the safety of the manor's interior, Victoria ascended the grand staircase, her skirts rustling softly against the polished wood. She entered her private sitting room, which afforded her a perfect view of the gardens below. Her gaze immediately found Thomas, his muscular body glistening with sweat as he worked diligently tending to the roses.

"Such a handsome devil," she thought, her fingers drumming against the windowsill. As she watched him, her imagination began to run wild with lustful thoughts. She saw herself drawing him into a heated embrace, their mouths exploring one another hungrily. They would tear away each other's clothes, exposing their most intimate parts to the cool garden air.

"God, how I want him," she whispered, her hand instinctively slipping beneath her petticoats, seeking relief for the growing ache between her legs. She could feel her own dampness, and without hesitation, she plunged her fingers into her throbbing folds.

"Thomas," she moaned softly, each stroke of her fingers sending delicious shivers down her spine. She imagined how his rough hands would feel on her body, how his lips would taste on her skin, and how his thick cock would fill her completely.

"Fuck me, Thomas," she gasped as her fantasy intensified, picturing him pounding into her with wild abandon, their bodies colliding in a symphony of pleasure. The thought of such vulgar acts being committed by a woman of her position only heightened the intensity of her arousal.

"Ah, fuck!" she cried out as her climax washed over her, her body convulsing with ecstasy. She leaned against the window, panting and flushed, her eyes still fixed on Thomas as he continued his work below, blissfully unaware of the sinful desires he had awakened within her.

"Tonight," she murmured to herself, determination setting in. "Tonight, I shall have him."

THE MOON CAST an ethereal glow over the manor, bathing Victoria's path in silver light as she crept silently down the hallway. Her heart pounded in her chest, a mixture of lust and trepidation coursing through her veins. The house was still, and she dared not make a sound for fear of alerting the staff.

"Tonight, my desires will be sated," she thought, her mind

replaying the earlier scene at the window, her fingers teasing herself to climax while watching Thomas work below. She had chosen a simple nightgown, foregoing her usual layers of petti-coats and corsets. It was both practical for her stealthy mission and for what she hoped would follow.

As she made her way to the cottages where the help slept, she saw him – Thomas, waiting for her, his eyes filled with the same fire she felt within her. He stood there in nothing but his trousers, his well-muscled chest exposed and gleaming under the moonlight.

"Ma'am," he whispered, grabbing her hand and leading her away from the cottages. They found a secluded spot in the garden, hidden by large shrubs and bathed in shadow. "I've been waiting for you."

"Thomas... I need you," she confessed, her voice quivering with desire. Without another word, they fell upon each other, their mouths meeting in a passionate, searing kiss that left them both breathless.

Thomas then lifted the hem of Victoria's nightgown and thrust his face between her legs. Victoria gasped as she felt Thomas's warm breath on her throbbing sex. His tongue darted out to taste her, and he hummed in approval. She couldn't believe she was doing this, but it felt so right. His hands gripped her hips tightly, and he slowly pushed her nightgown up to her waist, exposing her plump behind. He nudged her closer to the nearest tree trunk and began to lick and nip at the tender flesh of her buttocks, making soft moans escape her lips. Each bite sent shockwaves of pleasure throughout her body. She couldn't help but shiver and tremble under his skilled touch. Her fingers tangled in his hair, urging him on.

As he lapped at her juices with his rough tongue, his free hand snaked up her thigh, teasingly close to her aching pussy, but not quite touching it yet. She leaned back against the tree trunk, letting out a low moan as he continued his assault on her sensitive flesh. When he finally brushed his fingertips against her clit, she jolted forward, arching into his touch. He chuckled softly before sliding a finger inside of her wetness. Her walls clenched around his finger, pulling it deeper inside of her with each thrust of his tongue against her clit. Victoria's whole body tensed as she neared climax; she could feel it building quickly under his skilled ministrations.

"More...," she managed to choke out between gasps for air. He must have taken that as a sign because he relentlessly worked two fingers inside of her now while continuing to lick and suckle on her ass cheeks.

Thomas indulged in the flavors of her sex and her buttocks, lapping up her juices with his tongue and sucking on the area he knew drove her wild. Her sex twitched and pulsing against his lips as she was pushed ever closer to the edge of ecstasy. His fingers moved in and out, finding her G-spot, rubbing it in circles before pressing hard against it again and again, driving her crazier. Victoria's moans filled the night air, muffled only by the foliage around them. She tasted like heaven, and he couldn't get enough of her.

As she finally fell over the precipice into orgasm, she let out a long moan, hips bucking into his face as she came hard. He held onto her hips firmly to keep his mouth against her welcoming pussy as he lapped up every drop of her sweet release. When she subsided, he pulled his fingers from her hot depths and kissed his way up her thighs, nipping at the soft flesh of her inner thighs before capturing a particularly sensitive spot behind her knee and sucking gently. "Fuck," she panted out, still catching her breath.

"You taste so good," he praised between kisses, before standing up and pulling down his rough trousers with a grunt. His cock sprang free, already hard and ready for action. In one swift motion, he positioned himself at Victoria's entrance and plunged into her wet heat in one stroke, filling her completely. Her walls gripped him tightly as he started to move, their bodies slapping together in rhythm under the cover of darkness.

Victoria's heart raced as she felt Thomas's manhood sliding into her. Her mind was a whirlwind of sensations - the roughness of his skin against her own, the scent of him mingling with the earthy aroma of the garden. Each thrust sent waves of pleasure coursing through her body, and she arched her back to meet him. Their hips slapped together in a primal rhythm, their breathing forming a melody in the quiet night air. Her nails dug into his shoulders as he picked up speed, pounding into her with force, his hips undulating in a dance of desire.

She could feel herself getting close again, moaning into his neck as he gripped her tighter, pulling on her hair with roughly tender affection. He bit down softly on her bottom lip, drawing blood as she got closer to climaxing a second time. "Yeah, that's it," he growled against her ear, pushing deeper inside of her. The duke's widow's moans filled the darkness, and they were music to his ears.

She could feel every inch of him inside of her now, stretching and filling her completely. She clung onto him for dear life as he drove deeper still, her body shaking with pleasure. With one last deep thrust that sent shivers down both their spines, they climaxed together - Victoria's walls spasming around Thomas's cock while she screamed out in ecstasy beneath the canopy of stars above them. Thomas groaned loudly as he emptied himself into Victoria's womb slowly but powerfully; feeling every pulse of pleasure rippling through him as well.

As they caught their breaths after their frenzy subsided, Victoria rested against Thomas's chest. Spent, they collapsed onto the soft grass beneath them, their bodies still entwined. As their breathing slowed, Victoria looked into Thomas' eyes, her mind swirling with thoughts of primal lust and desire and a realization that she would never go back to being sexually unfulfilled again.

3

The sun had barely risen, casting a warm golden hue across the lush garden. Victoria, Duchess of Hawthorne, wandered through the maze of hedges and flowers, her heart pounding with anticipation. The previous night's encounter still lingered in her thoughts, sending shivers down her spine. She yearned to see Thomas again, to feel his touch and share in their secret passion.

"Ah, Your Grace!" called George, the head gardener, as he spotted Victoria from afar. His face was creased with excitement. "I have been meaning to introduce you to our newest employee."

Thomas emerged from behind a towering hedge, his muscular frame silhouetted against the morning light. He carried a basket of freshly picked roses, his hands roughened by days of labor. Victoria felt her pulse quicken as she feigned surprise at his presence.

"Your Grace," said George, "may I present Mr. Thomas Barrow, our new groundskeeper."

"Mr. Barrow," Victoria said, extending her hand for him to kiss, "it is a pleasure to make your acquaintance." Their eyes met, and it took every ounce of self-control not to reveal their secret rendezvous to George.

"Likewise, Your Grace," replied Thomas, his voice trembling ever so slightly. He bowed low before her, both excited and terrified at the prospect of being discovered by his employer.

"Mr. Barrow has already proven himself a skilled horticulturist," George beamed, proudly gesturing towards the beautiful rose bushes that seemed to flourish under Thomas' care. "He has a true gift."

"Indeed," Victoria murmured, her gaze fixated on Thomas. She could hardly believe that this man, who now appeared so innocent and humble, had taken her with such fervor just the night before. The very thought caused heat to rise within her, and she knew that she must find a way to be with him again.

"Your Grace, if you would like, I can take you on a tour of the garden's newest additions," suggested George, unaware of the dangerous game being played before his eyes.

"Thank you, George," Victoria replied, "but perhaps another time. I am certain that Mr. Barrow and I shall have many opportunities to discuss his work in the future."

"Of course, Your Grace," said George, bowing respectfully as he took his leave.

Once George was out of sight, Victoria turned to Thomas, her eyes pleading and apologetic. "Thomas, I must apologize for not telling you the truth about who I am," she whispered, her voice heavy with regret. "I never meant to deceive you, but our encounter happened so unexpectedly, and I... I couldn't bring myself to reveal my identity."

"Your Grace," Thomas murmured, his voice filled with a mix of confusion and desire. He ached to touch her again, to feel her naked body pressed against his as they had been just the night before. But he also knew that their situation had become infinitely more complicated now that he knew she was the Duchess.

"Please, call me Victoria," she insisted, stepping closer to him. The scent of roses hung in the air as their bodies drew near, the tension between them palpable. "And please, forgive me. Say that you can understand why I did what I did."

"Victoria," he whispered, allowing himself to take her hands in his, feeling her tremble beneath his touch. "I understand. And I forgive you. But we must be careful – both for your sake and mine."

"Thank you," she breathed, relieved at his understanding. Unable to resist any longer, she closed the distance between them and pressed her lips to his. Their mouths met with a hunger that could not be denied, tongues entwining as if trying to reclaim the passion that had been stolen from them by circumstance.

Thomas pulled her closer, his hands roaming over the curves of her body, seeking out the softness of her breasts beneath the folds of her dress. As he found what he sought, he moaned into their kiss, his fingers teasing her nipples until they were hard peaks begging for further attention.

"Touch me, Thomas," Victoria gasped, her voice thick with need. "Make me feel alive again."

He needed no further encouragement, his hands slipping beneath her skirts to find the wet heat waiting for him. His fingers traced over her swollen folds, slick with her desire, before seeking out the sensitive nub of her clit.

"Fuck," she moaned, her head falling back as he began to circle it with expert precision. "Yes, just like that."

"Your cunt's so wet for me, Victoria," Thomas whispered as he continued to stroke her, his own arousal growing with each breathy moan that escaped her lips. "I want to taste you on my tongue."

"Please," she begged, not caring about the impropriety of their actions – all that mattered was the pleasure they could bring to one another.

Thomas pulled away from their kiss for a moment and slid his hand between her legs, feeling the dampness soak through her clothes. His fingers found her clit and circled around it, teasing it gently as he looked into her eyes. She moaned in response, her lips parted and tongue darting out to wet them. Her eyes were heavy-lidded with desire as he slipped off one glove and then the other, setting them aside on the ground. Moving slowly so as not to alarm George or any of the other workers, he brought his fingers to his mouth and tasted her juices. The sweetness on his tongue made him moan as he sucked each one off, savoring every drop.

"You taste incredible," he breathed against her neck, his stubble scraping lightly against her soft skin. His other hand held onto the waist of her dress, trying to keep it from completely falling down as he ground himself against her, aching for more contact.

Victoria couldn't contain herself any longer; she pulled away from his mouth and ripped open the top of her dress, revealing her breasts to the crisp morning air. She arched into him, offering herself up while watching intently as Thomas' eyes traced the curves of her breasts before moving back up to meet hers again. She could feel him shaking with need next to her; it was intoxicating. He took one of her hard nipples into his mouth, sucking it gently between his teeth before soothing it with his tongue while pinching the other between two fingers and twisting lightly. She cried out softly into the quiet morning air as they stood there in the garden maze, lost in their own world of pleasure.

Victoria suddenly pulled away and knelt down in front of Thomas. She quickly pulled his trousers so that his cock sprung out. She reached out her hand and wrapped it around his throbbing shaft, stroking him slowly as she looked up at him with a mix of lust and curiosity. Her fingers were cold against his skin, but he could feel the heat emanating from her body as she gently stroked him. He closed his eyes, trying to prepare himself for what was about to happen. The heady scent of roses mixed with their arousal in the cool morning air.

Her lips brushed against the tip of his cock, teasing him softly before she finally engulfed it in her warm mouth. He gasped and let out a moan as she began to bob her head up and down, taking more of him into her mouth with each downward stroke. His hands found their way into her hair, tangling in the curls as he watched her work her magic on him. The sight of this powerful woman kneeling before him, taking him deep into her throat was enough to drive him wild.

Victoria teased him expertly, using both hands now to stroke and caress his length while she took more of him inside her mouth. She deep-throated him, hitting the back of her throat with each upstroke even as she moaned around him. Her tongue danced along the underside of his shaft, tasting every drop of pre-cum that leaked from the slit. She looked up at him with hooded eyes, meeting his gaze as she bobbed faster and harder.

Thomas' fingers dug into her shoulders as he tried to hold himself still for her pleasure. The sensation of her wet heat surrounding him was exquisite; but he didn't want to cum yet, so he pulled Victoria back up.

He stepped closer still, pushing their hips together so that their bodies rubbed against each other through their clothes, creating a friction that made them both gasp. He turned her around so that her back was against him. His hands slid down her trembling legs and up the insides of her thighs, and she parted them wider to invite him in. He groaned as he felt the hot wetness between them. She gasped as he slipped his cock inside her, her body welcoming him like a glove fitted just for him. With every thrust, she moaned louder than before, feeling him stretching her walls and filling her completely.

The scent of the roses mixed with their sweet sweat and the

heady floral perfume she wore, filling the air around them with an intoxicating aroma. He reached around to play with one of her nipples again while his other hand held onto the hedge behind her for support as he fucked her hard against it. The rough bark scratched at their skin but neither cared, lost in the sensation of this forbidden love making them both ache with desire. Every so often he'd pull out for a moment just to taste her again, lapping up the nectar that dribbled from her entrance, savoring every last drop.

As they moved faster together beneath the golden sunrise light filtering through the leaves above them, George's voice called out from afar - "Your Grace! Are you alright in there?"

Victoria froze momentarily before responding softly "I am fine thank you George! Just admiring the roses." Her pussy tightened around his cock, and he felt her walls clenching around him. He pulled out, turned her around and lifted her up so that she could wrap her legs around him. She kissed his neck hard, sucking a mark into his skin, her teeth lightly grazing the flesh, and her nails digging into his back. He growled at the feeling of being owned by this beautiful woman, his desire for her becoming even more intense with each passing moment. His cock pulsed inside her, ready to explode but he held back just as she did.

"You feel so good," he whispered into her ear before capturing it between his teeth, trailing a line of pleasure down its softness. The taste of her skin sent shivers down his spine. "Fuck," he groaned again, his body trembling as he drove deeper inside her. The sound of their flesh meeting filled the air, mingling with the birdsong and soft rustling of leaves around them. Victoria's moans echoed through the garden, each one louder than the last as he took control of their lovemaking while still giving her what she needed.

Her muscles quivered with anticipation as she felt him holding back from climaxing; it made their lovemaking all the more erotic for both of them. Every time he pulled out to taste her or tease her clit with his fingers, it sent waves of pleasure through her body that coursed up and down her spine, making every nerve ending tingle in delight. She arched into him with each thrust, begging for release but not wanting it either. She bit her lip hard as he reached between them once more to rub against her clit just right, sending shockwaves of pleasure coursing through every inch of her body.

Their movements became erratic as their lust overpowered any sense of reason or restraint as both of them came so hard they could barely stand. Quickly, they came back to their senses as they realized they were vulnerable to getting caught.

Thomas pulled away from Victoria, his heart beating wildly as he tried to catch his breath. He quickly put his gloves back on and adjusted his clothes. Victoria did the same, her face flushed red with a mix of exhilaration and embarrassment. They knew they had to act fast before George, who was the head gardener of the estate, discovered the secret affair with the Duchess.

"I need to make my way back to the manor now," Victoria whispered, her voice shaking with fear. "We cannot let anyone find out about this."

Thomas nodded, understanding the gravity of the situation. He gave Victoria a quick kiss and asked her to come see him again soon.

"Yes, my sweet," Victoria responded. "We will be together again soon."

EPILOGUE

Victoria entered the manor, her heart racing with a newfound sense of liberation. The grandiose staircase greeted her as she stepped into the foyer, its polished wooden railing gleaming in the candlelight. She ascended the stairs slowly, her mind awash with thoughts of her future.

"Perhaps..." she mused to herself, a wicked smile spreading across her full lips, "I need not be entirely miserable in life."

She glanced around at the opulent surroundings, her eyes lingering on the lavish tapestries and exquisite paintings adorning the walls. Her marriage to the elderly Duke had secured her a position in high society, but it had also deprived her of something far more precious - the wild, passionate experiences that set her heart ablaze. But now that he was gone, she was determined to set her own rules.

"Damn the societal norms," she whispered under her breath, her cheeks flushed with arousal as she recalled her recent tryst with Thomas. "There is so much more for me to explore... to taste... and to enjoy."

The realization dawned upon her like a radiant sun emerging

from behind the clouds; the world was truly her sexual playground.

"Who says I cannot indulge in my desires while still fulfilling my duties?" she thought, her pulse quickening as images of her encounters with Thomas flooded her mind – his strong hands caressing her supple skin, their bodies entwined in a dance of passion and lust. "There are so many other opportunities out there to explore my desires. I will make it my mission to find them"

As she reached the top of the staircase, Victoria paused for a moment to catch her breath before going to her bedchamber with a smile on her face.

ABOUT THE AUTHOR

Eliza Finch is a writer of short historical erotica. Check out some of her other work on Amazon and Kindle Unlimited.

All of Eliza's Books on Kindle Unlimited:
https://amazon.com/author/elizafinch

Sign up for Eliza's newsletter:
https://elizafinch.com

Get a FREE erotic short story by Eliza Finch, *Indebted to the Baron*:
https://BookHip.com/KBQKDNW

Printed in Great Britain
by Amazon

37030300R00020